For Sylvie—C. Rylant

Also for Sylvie—C. Robinson

Text copyright © 2016 by Cynthia Rylant
Jacket art and interior illustrations copyright © 2016 by Christian Robinson
All rights reserved. Published in the United States by Schwartz & Wade Books,
an imprint of Random House Children's Books,
a division of Penguin Random House LLC, New York.

Schwartz & Wade Books and the colophon are trademarks of Penguin Random House LLC.

Visit us on the Web! randomhousekids.com

Educators and librarians, for a variety of teaching tools, visit us at RHTeachersLibrarians.com

Library of Congress Cataloging-in-Publication Data is available upon request.
ISBN 978-0-553-50770-6 (hc) — ISBN 978-0-553-50771-3 (lib. bdg.)
ISBN 978-0-553-50772-0 (ebook)

The text of this book is set in Brandon Grotesque.
The illustrations were rendered in acrylic paint and cut paper collage.

MANUFACTURED IN CHINA
2 4 6 8 10 9 7 5 3 1
First Edition

words by
Cynthia Rylant

Little
PENGUINS

pictures by
Christian Robinson

schwartz & wade books • new york

Snowflakes?

Many
snowflakes.

Winter is coming!

Mittens?

Many mittens.

And matching scarves.

Socks?

One for each foot!

What about boots?

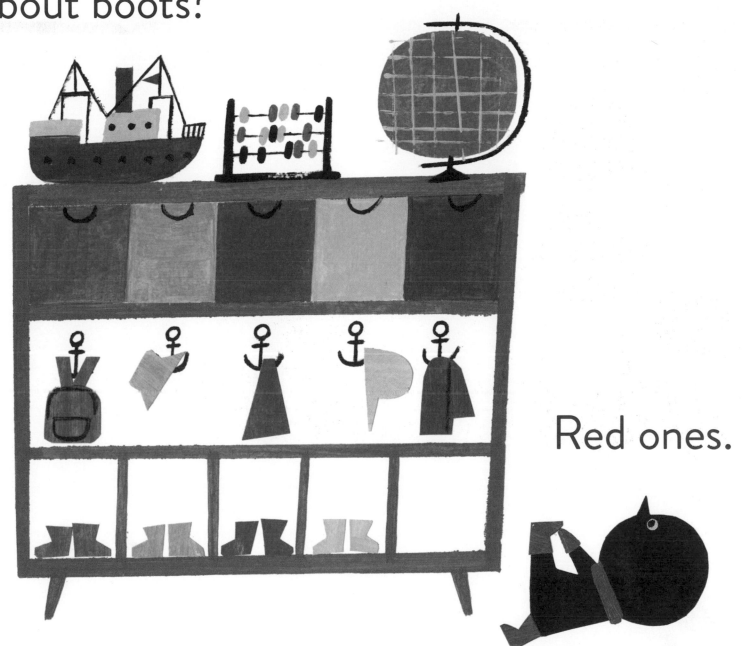

Red ones.

So, how's the snow?

Deep.

Deeper.

Very deep.

Where's Mama?

On her way!

Brrr. Let's go home.

off

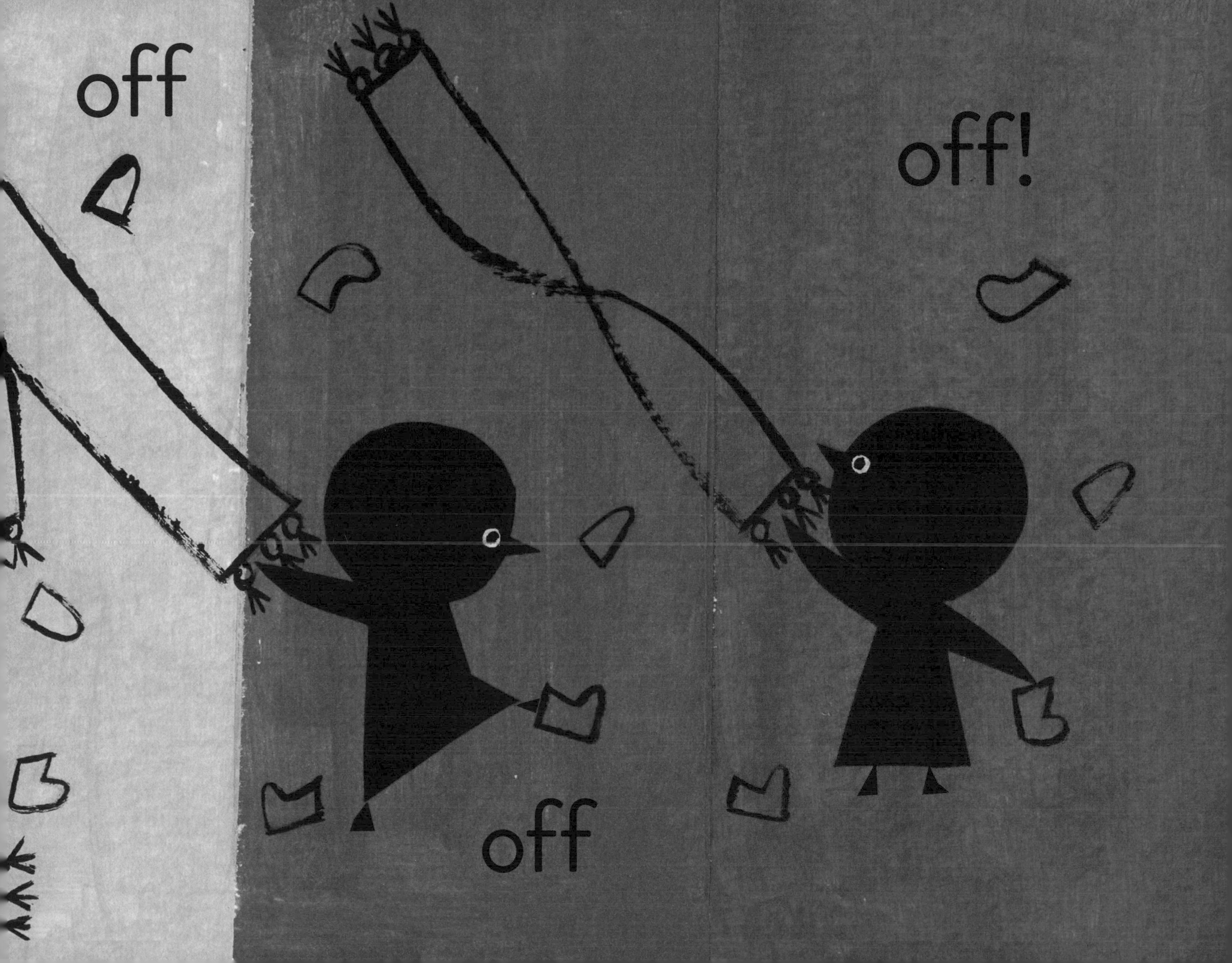

off

off!

Jammies on.

Warm cookies, please?

And sippies.

Thank you.

Wrap up tight.
Watch the night.

Winter is here.